MOBY DICK

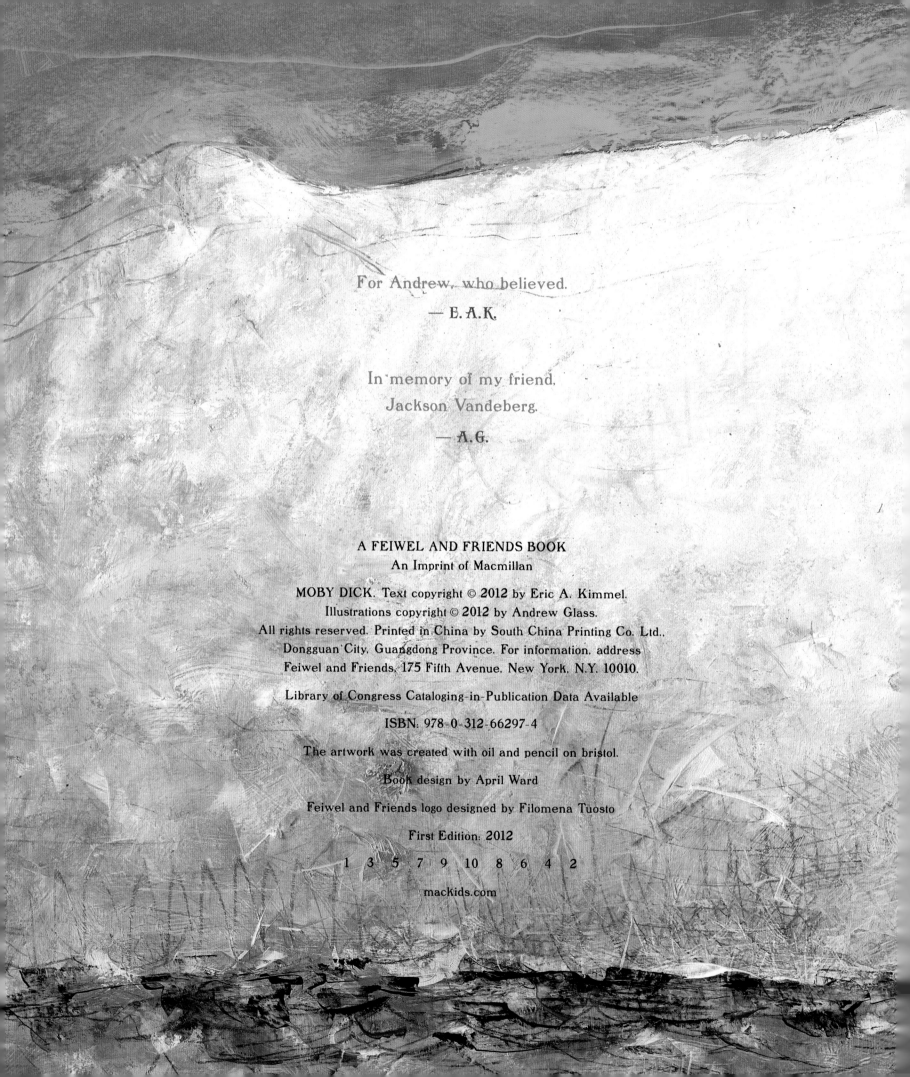

For Andrew, who believed.

— E. A. K.

In memory of my friend,
Jackson Vandeberg.

— A. G.

A FEIWEL AND FRIENDS BOOK
An Imprint of Macmillan

MOBY DICK. Text copyright © 2012 by Eric A. Kimmel.
Illustrations copyright © 2012 by Andrew Glass.

Library of Congress Cataloging-in-Publication Data Available

ISBN: 978-0-312-66297-4

The artwork was created with oil and pencil on bristol.

Book design by April Ward

Feiwel and Friends logo designed by Filomena Tuosto

First Edition: 2012

1 3 5 7 9 10 8 6 4 2

mackids.com

MOBY DICK

CHASING THE GREAT WHITE WHALE

ERIC A. KIMMEL

PAINTINGS BY
ANDREW GLASS

FEIWEL AND FRIENDS

NEW YORK

CALL ME ISHMAEL. . . .

When days start getting long again
and time is moving slow,
I set out for New Bedford town,
a'whaling for to go.

I checked into the Spouter Inn
and shared the only bed
with a harpooneer named Queequeg.
He had a tattooed head.

The *Pequod* was our whaler's name.
They seemed a jolly crew,
with Starbuck, Stubb, and Flash,
 the mates;
Tashtego and Daggoo.

Then Captain Ahab came on deck.
What happened to his leg?
T'was bitten off by Moby Dick.
That's why the whalebone peg.

"That parmacetti did me wrong.
I'll hunt him through the sea.
I promise when we meet again,
it's Moby Dick or me."

He nailed a doubloon to the mast
and said, "Look sharp and bold.
Whoever spies the White Whale first
will earn this Spanish gold."

Now, listen how to catch a whale.
We row up to its side,
then stick a harpoon in its back
and hang on for the ride.

We cut the blubber from the beast
and strip it to the bone.
So, in the end, Leviathan
makes oil for lamps at home.

Poor Queequeg started feeling sick
and none of us knew why.
We built a coffin just for him,
but then, he didn't die.

We scanned the ocean day by day
for any whale in sight.
We spied some blue and gray ones, too,
but not a single white.

"I seek the White Whale!" Ahab cried
to every passing ship.
Until the *Rachel* came in sight,
he'd given us the slip.

Their captain wept. "He took my boy.
Oh, help me find him, friend!"
Said Ahab, "Don't have time for boys.
My quest is near its end."

"It won't be long now," Ahab said.
"We're closing in. He knows."
Then from the mast, we heard the cry,

"AHOY, LADS! THAR, SHE BLOWS!"

His head rose high above the waves,
a Matterhorn of white.
The angle of his sickle jaw
gave everyone a fright.

We threw a harpoon at the whale
'fore he had time to blink.
He smacked our whaleboat with his tail
and tossed us in the drink.

Another day, we tried again.
Stubb yelled at us to row.
I saw a man caught in the lines
and carried down below.

On Moby's back, the dead man lay,
a'rising from the sea.
His arm swung out to beckon us,
"Oh, shipmates, follow me!"

Ahab stood, harpoon in hand.
His rage burned like the sun.
The weapon struck, a tangled line.
A shriek . . . and he was gone!

The whale smashed every single boat.
Enraged and furious,
he turned around, a Great White Mound,
and headed straight for us.

He rammed the *Pequod* with his head.
I heard the sighs and groans
of all my friends and shipmates
going down to Davy Jones.

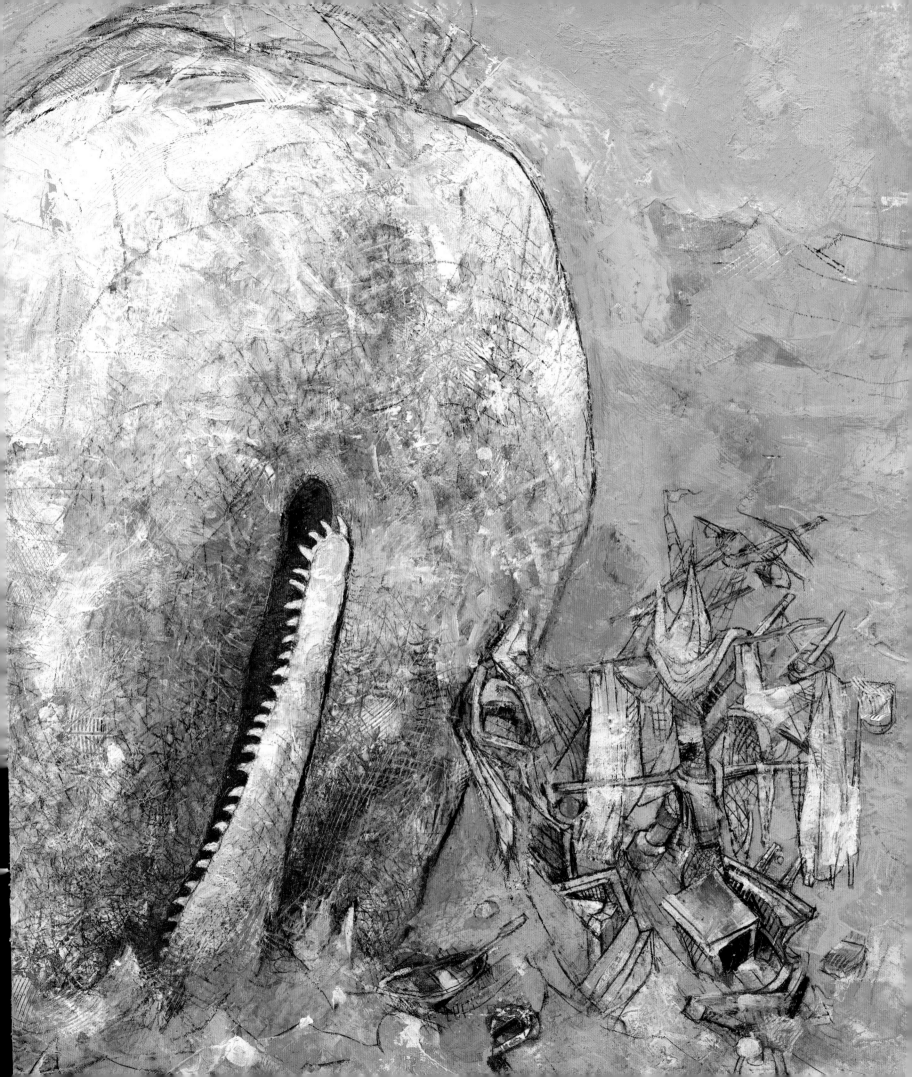

So, I am left to tell the tale
as, floating on the sea,
adrift in Queequeg's coffin box,
the *Rachel* rescued me.

The moral of this story is,
as my sad tale has shown:
Respect all creatures, great and small,
and leave the whales alone!

AUTHOR'S NOTE

MOBY DICK, the epic novel by American author Herman Melville (1819–1891), is considered to be one of the great works of world literature. The story is told by Ishmael, a sailor aboard the whaler *Pequod*, who recounts Captain Ahab's obsessive quest to hunt down the white sperm whale known as Moby Dick.

Moby Dick was first published in 1851 under the title *The Whale*. Melville based his story on an actual event. In 1820, the whaleship *Essex* was rammed and sunk by a sperm whale 2,000 miles off the western coast of South America. Eight members of the crew survived, but only after some had been reduced to eating the bodies of their dead shipmates. The *Essex*'s first mate, Owen Chase, published an account of the disaster, *The Narrative of the Most Extraordinary and Distressing Shipwreck of the Whale-Ship Essex*. Melville owned a copy of the book. He wrote notes to himself on the pages.

A second influence on Melville were news reports from Chile describing the hunting down and killing of a ferocious albino sperm whale known as Mocha Dick. Unlike other whales, Mocha Dick turned and attacked the whaleboats pursuing him. His body contained dozens of harpoons, tokens of his encounters with whalers.

Born and raised in New York City, Melville would later come to know his subject very well. His father, a successful merchant, made sure he received an excellent education. But the family business failed. Melville tried several careers: teacher, clerk, farmer, sailor. After seeking his fortune out west, he signed aboard the whaler *Acushnet* as an ordinary seaman. One of his goals in writing *Moby Dick* was to present a true picture of the men who worked the whale fishery. The American whaling industry was centered in the Massachusetts ports of Nantucket and New Bedford. At its peak, as many as 10,000 sailors served aboard whaleships that combed the remotest corners of the Southern Atlantic and Pacific Oceans, hunting whales for the oil that fueled the lamps and lubricated the machinery of nineteenth-century America.

For some readers, Captain Ahab was a hero; to others, he was just crazy. But for everyone, *Moby Dick* is a tragic and fearsome story—as instructive and compelling today as it was when it was first written.

GLOSSARY OF TERMS

Blubber: A special tissue containing fat and blood vessels that allows whales to dive deep and survive cold temperatures. Blubber was melted down to make valuable whale oil.

Davy Jones: In sailor legend, the ruler of the ocean. Drowned sailors are said to have "gone to Davy Jones' Locker."

Doubloon: A Spanish gold coin, minted in Mexico or Peru. Nineteenth-century Americans often used coins from other countries.

Drink: Another way of saying, "the ocean."

Harpoon: A barbed lance attached to ropes secured to the whaleboat. Harpoons were thrown into the whale's body. The frightened whale would try to swim away, dragging the whaleboats behind until it was exhausted and easy to kill. Whaling was and is a cruel business.

Harpooneer: A sailor who had the challenging task of throwing a harpoon into the whale. Harpooneers had high status aboard whaleships because of their courage and skill.

Leviathan: In the Bible and in Hebrew legend, Leviathan is the gigantic fish who rules the ocean. Whales are called leviathans because of their size.

Matterhorn: A famous European mountain. The Matterhorn is one of the highest peaks in the Swiss Alps.

Parmacetti: A sailor's way of saying "spermacetti." A spermacetti is a sperm whale.

Sickle jaw: Moby Dick's jaw had a curved shape because of a birth defect.

Whalebone peg: Whaleship carpenters used the bones of whales as substitutes for wood. Captain Ahab's "peg leg" was made from whalebone.

Whaler: A ship specially designed for the whaling industry. Whalers went on long voyages to the remotest parts of the ocean. They had to be strongly built and big enough to carry a large crew and supplies for a voyage that might last years. Whalers also needed extra storage space to hold hundreds of barrels of whale oil if the voyage was successful.